**FRIENDS
OF ACPL**

Hannah's Bookmobile Christmas

SALLY DERBY

with pictures by

GABI SWIATKOWSKA

Henry Holt and Company —⌒ New York

Henry Holt and Company, LLC
Publishers since 1866
115 West 18th Street
New York, New York 10011

Henry Holt is a registered trademark of Henry Holt and Company, LLC
Text copyright © 2001 by Sally Derby
Illustrations copyright © 2001 by Gabi Swiatkowska
All rights reserved.
Published in Canada by Fitzhenry & Whiteside Ltd., 195 Allstate Parkway, Markham, Ontario L3R 4T8.

Library of Congress Cataloging-in-Publication Data
Derby, Sally.
Hannah's bookmobile Christmas / Sally Derby; pictures by Gabi Swiatkowska.
Summary: Blue Bird the bookmobile provides shelter on a snowy Christmas Eve night.
[1. Christmas—Fiction. 2. Bookmobiles—Fiction. 3. Snow—Fiction.]
I. Swiatkowska, Gabi, ill. II. Title.
PZ7.D4416 Bl 2001 [E]—dc21 00-44857
ISBN 0-8050-6420-6
Designed by Martha Rago / First Edition—2001
The artist used acrylic on illustration board to create the illustrations for this book.
Printed in the United States of America on acid-free paper. ∞
1 3 5 7 9 10 8 6 4 2

With love to Michael,
who would make a splendid bookmobile driver
—S. D.

For Jessica and Žak
—G. S.

*S*nowflakes like dandelion fluff floated in the air. Christmas carols rang through the streets, and the sleigh bells on Blue Bird's door chimed merrily as people went in and out. Tonight would be Christmas Eve and everyone was happy. Everyone but Mary—she was worried. After all, Blue Bird was getting old.

Mary and Blue Bird had a history together. In 1970 Blue Bird, shiny and new, became Wadsworth's first bookmobile. With pictures of books and children on her sides and the name *Blue Bird* above her grille, she could carry over four thousand books. Mary climbed behind the wheel as the town's first bookmobile driver-librarian. "I love books and I love driving," Mary had said. "I've found the perfect job!" That was a long time ago. Now Blue Bird was very old for a bookmobile, and Mary's ginger curls had streaks of gray.

"Why are you frowning, Aunt Mary?" asked Hannah, Mary's eight-year-old niece and helper.

"We've a lot of stops today," Mary said. "All over town, and then up Devil's Backbone to drop you off at home. If it snows too heavily, we'll never make it up the hill. And wouldn't it be a shame if you couldn't get home on Christmas Eve!"

Hannah looked through the windshield at the flakes drifting like feathers. She picked up Dickens, Mary's cat, who was named after Mary's favorite writer. Dickens had his own special basket near Mary's seat, and now he jumped into it from Hannah's arms. "What do you think, Dickens?" Hannah asked, watching him wash his paws. "Maybe the snow won't stick."

But as Mary drove into the post office parking lot, the snow started falling in earnest. Sarah Conroy, snowflakes on her eyelashes, climbed up Blue Bird's steps first.

"Hello, Hannah," she said. "What a lucky girl you are to have a job at your age."

"I just help out for fun," Hannah said. "Otherwise I'd be stuck at the top of Devil's Backbone with no one to play with the whole Christmas vacation." She held out her hand to Mrs. Conroy. "Here, give me your book and I'll check it in."

Mrs. Conroy had picked out her books and was almost ready to leave when she stopped and turned back to Hannah. "I almost forgot," she said, reaching into the deep pocket of her jacket and pulling out a gaily patterned Christmas tin. "Party mix from Fred and me. We always make some for Christmas."

After Mrs. Conroy, bookmobile visitors came steadily till Mary's time at the post office was almost up. "When will Sol Eichberg get here?" Mary worried aloud. "I don't want to leave before he comes."

Just then Mr. Eichberg, the local writer, came hurrying out of the post office. "Hi, Mary. Hi, Hannah. Merry Christmas! I'm glad I didn't miss you."

Mr. Eichberg was one of Hannah's favorite people. Tall, with hair the color of paprika and eyebrows like upside down Vs, he always dressed in black. Sometimes he came to Hannah's school and read stories that he had written.

"That's okay, Sol," Mary said. "But with a blizzard coming, we can't afford to get behind schedule."

"The radio says the forecast is for six to eight inches."

"I hope not. At the end of the day I have to take Hannah up Devil's Backbone. That's one tough hill even without snow."

"Well, if you get stuck you can sit back and eat some of my *schnecken*," Mr. Eichberg said, handing a foil-wrapped package to Mary.

"You didn't need to give me a present," Mary protested. "But I won't say no to German pastries, that's for sure."

When she and Hannah drove away from the post office, Mary cast a worried look out the window. The clouds loomed lower and darker than ever, and Blue Bird's headlights probed through a whirlwind of snow. Under the tires, the road was slushy and wet. "Accident weather," Mary murmured. "We'll have to be careful today, Blue Bird."

"I'm not worried," Hannah said, pushing her bangs back from her face. "Daddy says he doesn't know anyone who can drive as well as you."

At the nursery school, the boys and girls held their books in mittened hands. They clambered aboard cheerfully, and for half an hour Blue Bird's narrow aisle was full of the chatter of children as they picked out their books. Outside, the wind whistled and the day grew darker. The playground swings had thick seats of white.

When the last child left, Mary swung Blue Bird's front door shut and headed up Main Street. She peered out the window at the trees bending in the wind. Their branches seemed to clutch at sheets of blowing snow. "I don't like the way it looks," Mary said. "Not a bit." Even Hannah was a little worried now.

The next stop was Chad Worth's house. Mary honked the horn gently. Chad's front door opened, and Chad wheeled himself slowly down his ramp. The wheels of his chair turned white, and they left narrow tracks in the snow. Mary got the chairlift ready. In a second she had Chad inside.

"Hey, Mary. Hey, Hannah. Isn't this great? Snow for Christmas! Got any new mysteries?"

"Wait a minute," said Hannah, searching through the box of returned books. "Here, I bet you'll like this one. I just read it

last week." She handed a small paperback book to Chad.

"I made some fudge for you, Hannah," Chad said, blushing a little. "We always make fudge to give away for Christmas."

"Thank you! I love fudge," Hannah answered.

After Chad picked out his books, it was time for Blue Bird to move on.

The road under Blue Bird's wheels was slippery now. Few cars were out. Under caps of snow, the headlights shone out like frightened eyes.

The snow flew thicker and faster. Still, at every stop a few people waited. Mothers with their babies bundled up in blankets. Farmers in blue jeans and ski jackets. More boys and girls out of school for Christmas vacation. And at every stop someone seemed to have a gift for Mary and Hannah. Crackers and cheese, nuts and cookies, and rolls of Christmas sausage piled up in the space between their seats.

At the last stop before Hannah's, three-year-old Josh Melville pulled away from his mother's hand and scrambled up Blue Bird's steps, taking time to give the sleigh bells an extra ring. "Did you get it?" he asked Mary, his dark eyes shining. "Did you get a book about Santa Claus?"

"I saved one specially for you," said Mary. Josh's mother and Mary talked about the roads and the snow and what the weatherman was saying, while Hannah and Josh looked at his new book and petted Dickens.

Finally Mary said, "I sure hope I can drop Hannah off at home. But I'm wondering if Blue Bird can make it. Devil's Backbone is treacherous. All those curves and twists will be ice-slick by now."

"Hannah can spend the night with us if you can't get her home," said Josh's mother. "But I suppose she'd rather celebrate Christmas Eve with her family."

Hannah smiled shyly at her. "Thanks, but I really do want to get home," she said quietly.

"Well then." Josh's mother opened a bag she had hanging from her arm. "Here's a little present for you and Mary." She handed them two Christmas tins. "Christmas cookies and my cocoa mix. If you get stranded, at least you'll have something to eat and drink," she laughed merrily.

Mary laughed too. "I don't think we'll starve," she said, pointing to their pile of gifts.

So Blue Bird plowed on. The big old bookmobile crept up the lower stretch of Devil's Backbone. Mary turned the windshield wipers on high, but the snow covered the windows almost as fast as the wipers could fan it away. A patch of ice surprised Mary, and Blue Bird skidded. "Hold on there, old girl," she said, gripping the steering wheel. "It's a long way to the top."

Little by little, curve by curve, Blue Bird inched up the hill. Outside, the afternoon was almost dark. Lights gleamed here and there from houses on the hillside.

"We may get up, but will I get back down?" Mary asked herself. Hannah chewed nervously on one of her braids. Blue Bird's motor strained, her exhaust pipe coughed puffs of smoke. "Just a bit more," Mary said.

All of a sudden the rear of the bookmobile fishtailed. Blue Bird slid sideways. "Not into the ditch!" Mary gasped, easing up on the accelerator. Blue Bird's rear kept sliding closer and closer to the ditch. Hannah put a hand on the dashboard to steady herself. Then, at the last possible moment, the bookmobile straightened out.

Mary laughed shakily. "Thought we were goners there, for a minute," she said to Hannah.

"I knew you could do it," Hannah answered stoutly.

Finally Blue Bird neared Hannah's mailbox. Mary and Hannah looked out the window. The long, bumpy lane that led to Hannah's house stretched off through the gathering darkness.

"Blue Bird and I better drive you up the lane," Mary said slowly.

"Oh, no!" Hannah protested. "Not even Blue Bird could make it today. You know there's mud under the snow. Dad's always saying we should move, especially when the weather gets like this and he can't drive to work. I'll just walk the rest of the way." As Hannah spoke, a spattering of sleet pelted against Blue Bird's windshield, and a gust of wind shook her frame.

"No, you won't," Mary said. "It's not usually a bad walk, but in the dark with snow on the ground and sleet in the air, I couldn't let you walk home."

"Well, I can't just stay here," Hannah said.

At that, Mary clapped her hands and smiled. "Why not?" she asked. "Blue Bird can't make it back down the hill—not in this. And it isn't fit weather to try to get back to your house. Why don't you and Dickens and I spend the night in Blue Bird? She's snug and warm."

"And we've got all sorts of things to eat and drink. We can make cocoa in your electric teapot!" piped Hannah. "The snow's sure to stop by morning. Then we can both walk back home for breakfast and open our presents to each other."

Just as Hannah finished speaking, the clank of tire chains could be heard, and headlights approached. A car stopped behind them and a door slammed.

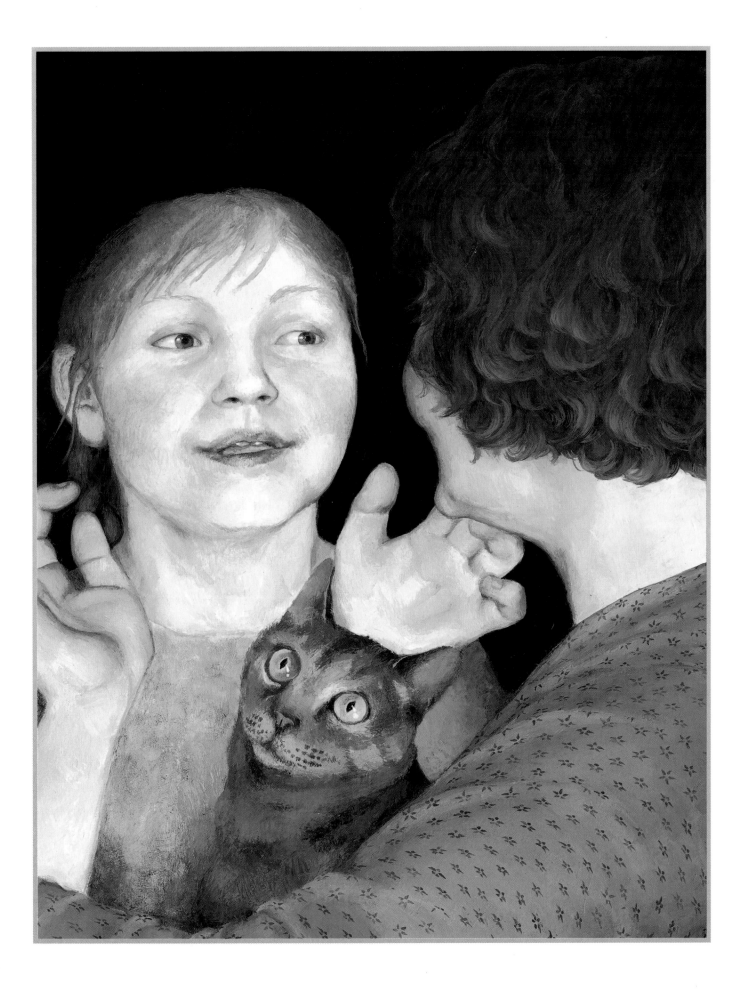

In a minute, Bob Williams, the sheriff, knocked on Mary's side window. "Hi, there, Mary. Is Blue Bird stuck?"

"As good as," Mary admitted. "I'm afraid to try to make it back down the hill, or up the lane to Hannah's house. We're thinking of spending the night here."

"Sure you don't want to hop in the cruiser and ride back to town with me?" Sheriff Williams asked. "I won't try that lane of yours, Hannah, but I'd be glad to take you and Mary to town."

"I'm sure," said Hannah, and "No, thanks," said Mary at the same time.

"But when you get to a phone, will you call and tell my folks where I am so my mom won't worry?" Hannah asked.

"Be glad to. The snow is supposed to stop soon. I'll drive by to check on you a couple of times during the night. Merry Christmas, then."

"Merry Christmas to you, too," answered Mary.

As the sheriff left, Mary looked at Hannah. "You really won't miss having Christmas Eve at home, Hannah?"

"Not as long as I get back tomorrow morning to open my gifts," Hannah said. "I'm sorry I'll miss church, but even if I was at home, we couldn't make it there in this weather. Pastor Behrens will understand, don't you think?"

"Sure he will," Mary answered.

After a while, the snow did stop falling. The lights of houses glowed on a world of white. Late in the evening, church bells pealed through the night air, and all over Wadsworth, people looked out at the snow, saying to one another, "A white Christmas! What a perfect night for snuggling up with a Christmas story."

And up on Devil's Backbone, safe and cozy in Blue Bird, that's exactly what Mary and Hannah were doing.

KARL MILLER

Afterword

"Here comes the bookmobile!" Across the United States, readers have been calling out those excited words for more than ninety years. Ever since 1905, when the first horse-drawn "book wagon" rolled along the roads of Washington County, Maryland, bookmobiles have been bringing books and magazines to eager readers. At the height of their popularity there were more than two thousand bookmobiles operating in the United States.

In the 1970s, concern over the cost and availability of gasoline caused many to conclude that bookmobiles were a thing of the past, but in recent years they are being rediscovered as a welcome way to bring together books and readers. Today, in addition to books and magazines, the bookmobile may carry videos and compact discs. Some even have a computer for the librarian to use. Big cities like Little Rock, Arkansas, and Dallas, Texas, are sending the rolling libraries to senior citizen and day-care centers, to housing projects and city parks.

So keep your eyes out. Someday you too may be able to cry, "Here it comes! Here comes the bookmobile!"